DREAMWORKS

HOW TO TRAIN YOUR DRAGON 2

Dragon Race!

by Cordelia Evans

SIMON SPOTLIGHT
An imprint of Simon & Schuster Children's Publishing Division
New York London Toronto Sydney New Delhi
1230 Avenue of the Americas, New York, New York 10020
How To Train Your Dragon 2 © 2014 DreamWorks Animation L.L.C.
SIMON SPOTLIGHT and colophon are registered trademarks of Simon & Schuster, Inc.
For information about special discounts for bulk purchases, please contact Simon & Schuster Special Sales
at 1-866-506-1949 or business@simonandschuster.com.
Manufactured in the United States of America 0314 NGS
First Edition 10 9 8 7 6 5 4 3 2
ISBN 978-1-4814-0474-7
ISBN 978-1-4814-2578-0 (eBook)

Welcome, ladies and gentlemen, to the event you've all been waiting for since . . . well, since last time we did this: today's dragon race! I'm Stoick, chief of the Vikings on the island of Berk, and I'll be your announcer for the race.

Gathered at the starting line we have all the best dragon racing teams in Berk: Astrid and Stormfly, Snotlout and Hookfang, Ruffnut and Tuffnut and Barf and Belch, Fishlegs and Meatlug, and . . . Hiccup and Toothless are nowhere to be found. What am I going to do with my son?

And they're off! Look at those dragons fly—they are streaming above rooftops and between buildings at an amazing speed. A few laps into the race, and I see a cluster of sheep hiding between two buildings over there waiting to be snatched up. Let's see if any of our racers spot them too!

It looks like Fishlegs and good old Meatlug have picked up a sheep. Meatlug's great hovering ability often helps her zero in on the prize, and—what's this? Wow, we have an upset! Snotlout and Hookfang have stolen Fishlegs's sheep, and they've . . . they've given it to Ruffnut?! What is going on here?!

We're still unclear about that sheep gift, but the race is continuing at a fast pace. The teams are rounding the bend, heading through the stables, and right back toward the arena. That means it's time, last lap. Sound the horn! Launch the black sheep! There it goes. It's sailing through the air. Up and up and up. Looks like Astrid is going to catch it!

Wow, a surprise attack from above, and Fishlegs captures the sheep once again! But this time, *he's* given it to Ruffnut! That girl has won the heart of every young man in Berk, it seems!

Now it looks like the twins are fighting over the sheep. Should someone tell them they're on the same team? No? Are they going to sabotage themselves here after practically being *given* this victory? Ah, here we go! We've got Astrid coming in quickly toward the twins. She's narrowing in. They don't see her, and . . . yes! She's stolen the sheep! *That's* my future daughter-in-law!

Astrid has almost reached the finish line, but it looks like there'll be one more attempt to thwart her before she can win. Snotlout and Fishlegs are closing in on both sides. Don't let them steal it, Astrid. They're just going to give it to Ruffnut anyway! Ah, thatta girl, she's escaped Snotlout's hammer—which looks like it's unfortunately caught Fishlegs in the face—and the black sheep goes into Astrid's basket. Astrid takes the game!

Whew, that was an exciting race! But how did we come to fly and race dragons in Berk, you ask? Well, you see, dragons used to be our enemies. We lived in fear of them and fought them as best we could. But that was before my son Hiccup met his dragon Toothless and trained him. Now dragons and Vikings live peacefully together on Berk, and our favorite new pastime is dragon racing.

RULES OF DRAGON RACING

Now that you've seen our competitors in action, let's go over the actual rules of dragon racing. (Not that they're set in stone . . .)

- First a pack of sheep is released.

- As the racers fly laps around town, their goal is to catch as many sheep as possible and make it back to the arena to deposit the sheep in their baskets—before another racer steals them!

- Each sheep in a racer's basket is worth one point.

- On the last lap Gobber loads a black sheep into the catapult and launches it into the arena.

- The racer who catches the black sheep and deposits it safely into his or her basket is awarded a whopping ten points! This frequently makes this racer the winner, but not always!

Let's meet the best dragon racing teams in Berk!

HICCUP AND TOOTHLESS

TEAM TOOTHLESS

RANK: 1

WINS: 15

POINTS: 460

DRAGON SPECIES: NIGHT FURY

CLASS: STRIKE

ABILITY: DIVE BOMB

WINGSPAN: 45 FEET

AVERAGE SPEED: 80 MPH

RIDER: HICCUP

Hiccup is Berk's champion racer despite his missing leg and his dragon's injured tail. He's constantly inventing and practicing new flying tricks and techniques which help lead him to victory. Plus he's more quick-witted than most, so he can stay ahead of the competition.

DRAGON: TOOTHLESS

Hiccup's dragon and best friend, Toothless, is the only Night Fury known to Berk, and the fastest dragon alive. He can't fly without Hiccup, but because he trusts his rider completely, he's the best flyer in Berk.

ASTRID AND STORMFLY

TEAM STORMFLY

RANK: 2

WINS: 10

POINTS: 357

DRAGON SPECIES: NADDER

CLASS: TRACKER

ABILITY: SPINE SHOT

WINGSPAN: 42 FEET

AVERAGE SPEED: 75 MPH

RIDER: ASTRID

Right on the tail of Team Toothless is Team Stormfly. Rider Astrid is as tough as they come, and she doesn't give up a race without a fight. Her bravery and daring when trying out new stunt maneuvers make her an excellent strategic racer.

DRAGON: STORMFLY

Deadly Nadders like Stormfly may be beautiful, and you can pet them, but avoid their tails—they are extremely sharp to the touch. A fast, elegant flyer, Stormfly is a perfect dragon for Astrid, as she's just as strong-willed and determined to give Hiccup and Toothless a run for their money.

SNOTLOUT AND HOOKFANG

TEAM HOOKFANG

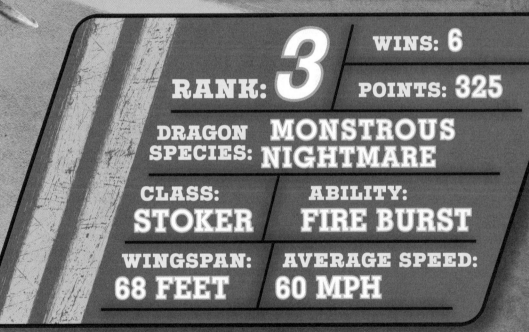

RANK: **3**

WINS: 6

POINTS: 325

DRAGON SPECIES: **MONSTROUS NIGHTMARE**

CLASS: **STOKER**

ABILITY: **FIRE BURST**

WINGSPAN: **68 FEET**

AVERAGE SPEED: **60 MPH**

RIDER: SNOTLOUT

Snotlout is one of the strongest Vikings in Berk—and he knows it! He's extremely determined to win and always pushes himself to the limit. Sometimes his stubbornness and overconfidence can get him in trouble, though, and when he loses, he does *not* handle it well.

DRAGON: HOOKFANG

Hookfang has a huge wingspan, making him a superfast flyer. He can burst into flames, which is more useful in battle than during a race, but can still come in handy from time to time. Hookfang can be as hotheaded as his rider, and when he and Snotlout don't agree, any chance they have at winning goes up in flames. . . literally!

FISHLEGS AND MEATLUG

TEAM MEATLUG

RANK: 4

WINS: 4

POINTS: 280

DRAGON SPECIES: GRONCKLE

CLASS: BOULDER

ABILITY: LAVA BLAST

WINGSPAN: 18 FEET

AVERAGE SPEED: 65 MPH

RIDER: FISHLEGS

If you could win a race with enthusiasm and knowledge about dragons, Fishlegs would win every time! He loves Meatlug just as much as Hiccup loves Toothless, and tries his best to keep her safe at all times. He's a "slow and steady wins the race" sort of guy, but he doesn't often win the race.

DRAGON: MEATLUG

Meatlug spends a lot of time sleeping. After all, she needs to rest up if she's going to race Toothless, Stormfly, and the other dragons! She may not be the fastest dragon, but her ability to spit flaming lava and her thick, protective skin help keep her in the running during a race, and her hovering skills are a huge advantage when it comes to catching sheep.

RUFF & TUFF
BARF & BELCH

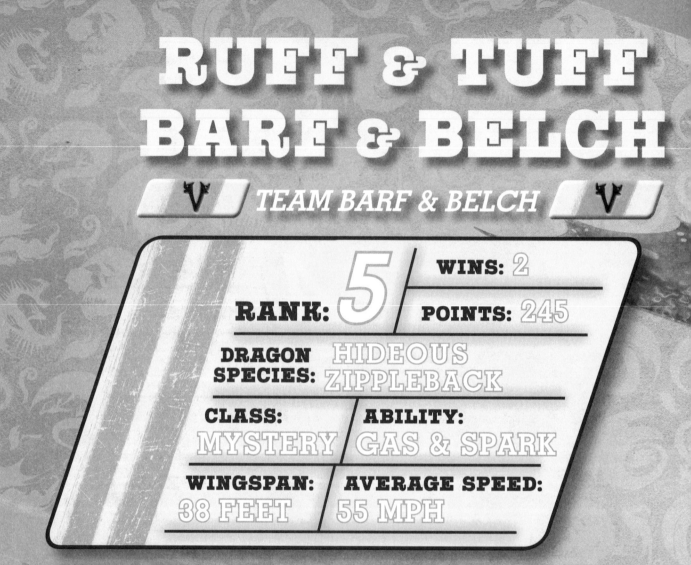

TEAM BARF & BELCH

RANK: 5

WINS: 2

POINTS: 245

DRAGON SPECIES: HIDEOUS ZIPPLEBACK

CLASS: MYSTERY

ABILITY: GAS & SPARK

WINGSPAN: 38 FEET

AVERAGE SPEED: 55 MPH

RIDERS: RUFF & TUFF

Twins Ruffnut and Tuffnut love the adrenaline and excitement that comes with racing dragons. Competitive in general but most competitive with each other, Ruff and Tuff are good racers when they can agree on a plan, but they usually don't! This is what most often prevents them from winning.

DRAGONS: BARF & BELCH

Barf and Belch are silent, stealthy racers— when they're working together, that is. Like their bickering riders, their sometimes conflicting instincts can cause them to stall in the middle of a race. Ruffnut rides Barf who produces gas and Tuffnut rides Belch who produces the spark. The two elements combine to create a massive explosion.

It's time for another race. Hiccup and Toothless have returned from exploring to give everyone a run for their money. Okay, come on up to the starting line, racers. Everybody ready? Three, two, one, and they're off! May the best team win!